For Oscar Belfrage Bordoli ~ M.M

For Fay B. with love ~ M.McQ

BARE BEAR
by Miriam Moss and Mary McQuillan

British Library Cataloguing in Publication Data

A catalogue record of this book is available
from the British Library.

ISBN 0340 88203 4 PB

First edition published 2005

Paperback edition first published 2006

10 9 8 7 6 5 4 3 2 1

Published by Hodder Children's Books,
a division of Hodder Headline Limited,
338 Euston Road, London, NW1 3BH

Printed in China

Bare Bear

Written by
Miriam Moss

Illustrated by
Mary McQuillan

Hodder
Children's
Books

A division of Hodder Headline Limited

Busby, a small brown
bouncy young bear,
lived deep in the mountains
in a neat little lair.

One night as he slept
a stormy wind blew,
snatched his clothes
off the line...

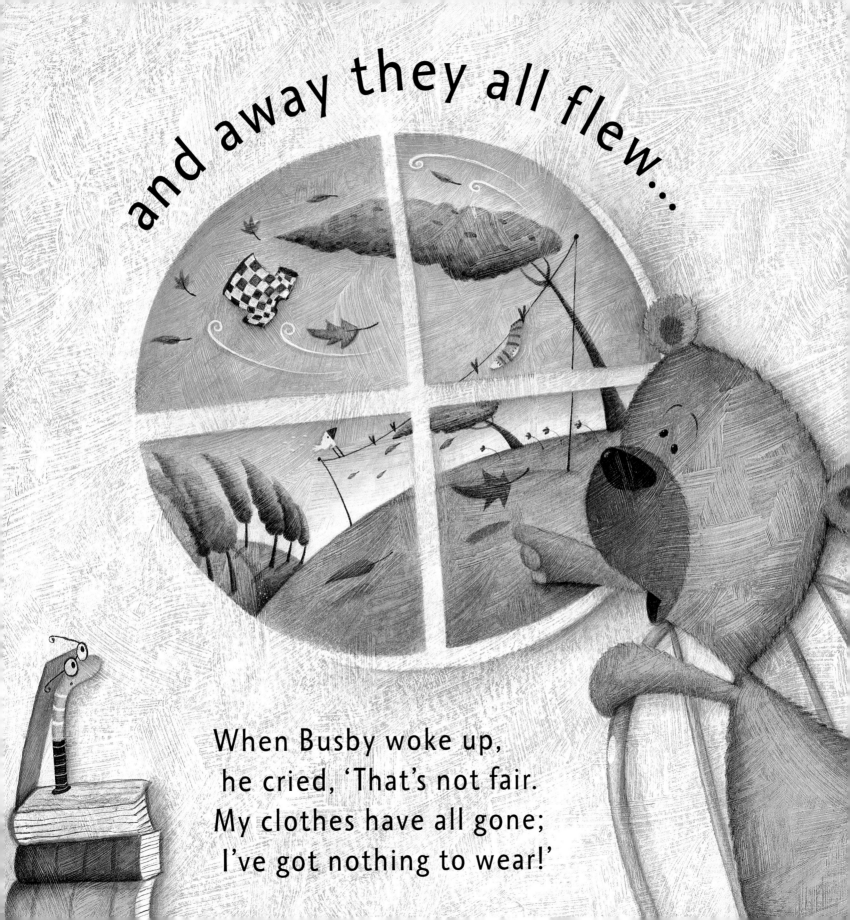

and away they all flew...

When Busby woke up,
he cried, 'That's not fair.
My clothes have all gone;
I've got nothing to wear!'

Busby looked in the garden,
then in the wild wood,
and there stood a hare
in a red riding hood!

In her basket she carried
a checked cloth,
a fruit flan,
and a small ginger cake
to share with her gran.

'Excuse me,' said Busby,
'I'm sure you know best,
but that cloth in your basket
looks just like my vest.

Last night as I slept
a stormy wind blew,
snatched my clothes off the line
and away they all flew.'

Hare held up the cloth,
'Yes, I see you're undressed!
You **are** short of clothes;
let me help find the rest.'

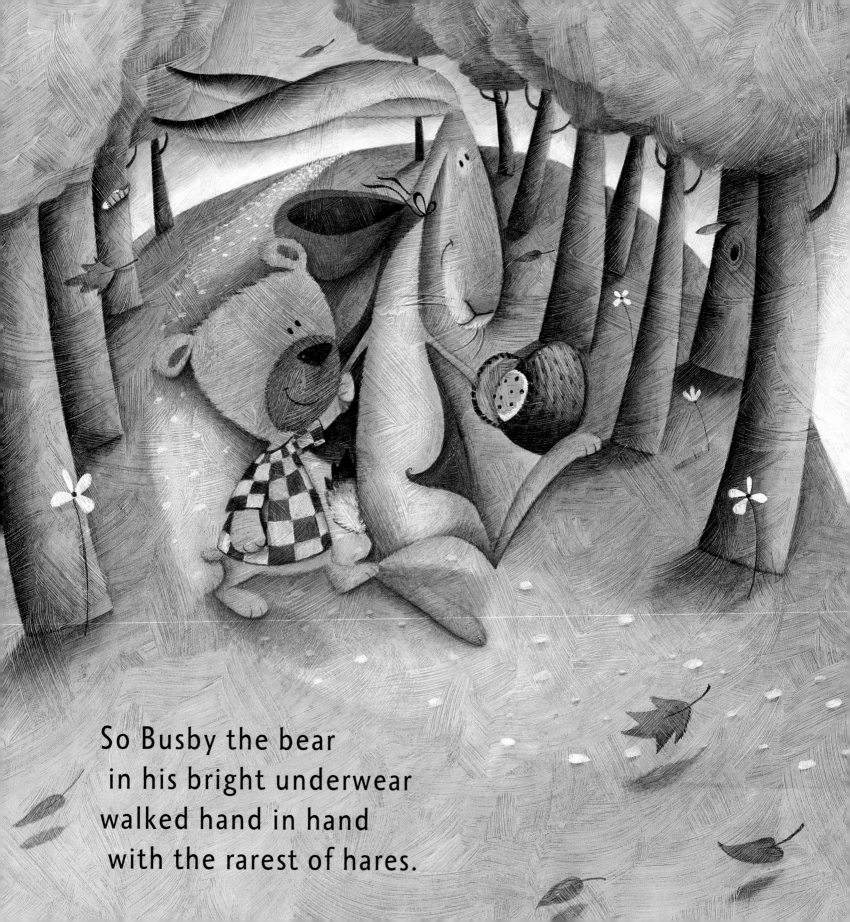

So Busby the bear
in his bright underwear
walked hand in hand
with the rarest of hares.

They searched high and low.
They looked everywhere.

They walked in a circle,
and then in a square...

BOING! BOING!

Leaning out of a house
that was clearly a clock
was a mouse who was holding
a striped yellow sock.

Then he started to use it
to polish the clock!

The clock went 'TICK
TOCK,'
as the bear went 'KNOCK
KNOCK!'

and the mouse he ran down
to unfasten the lock.

'Excuse me,' said Busby.
'I think that it's time
to mention right now
that THAT sock is

MINE.'

Mouse held up his duster,
'Yes, I see you're undressed!
You **are** short of clothes;
let me help find the rest.'

So the rarest of hares
and the mouse with no clock
walked hand in hand
with the bear in one sock.

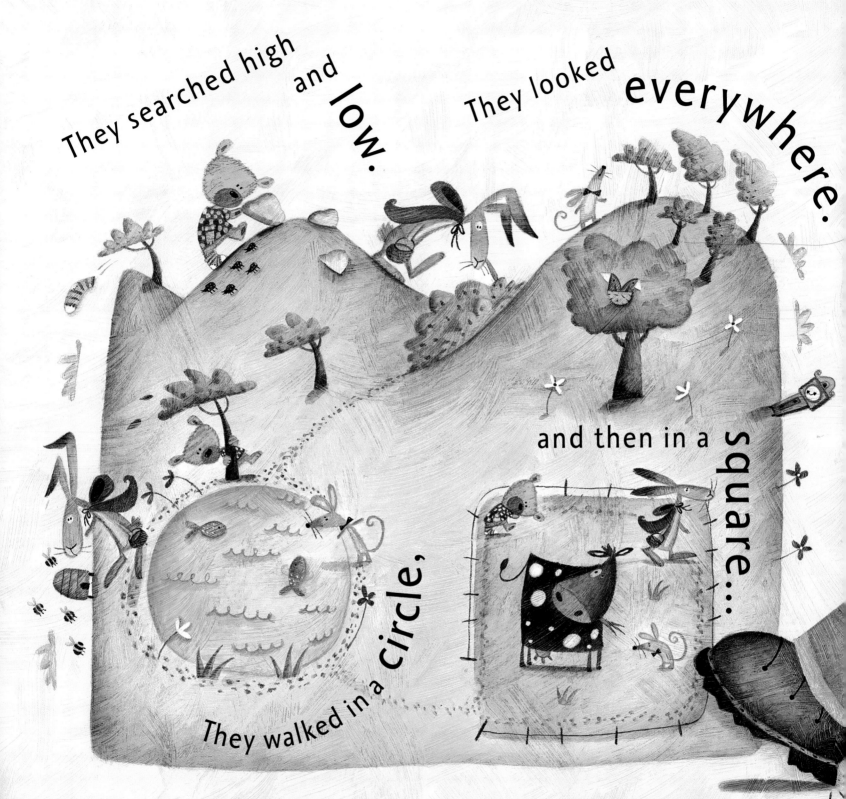

They searched high and low. They looked everywhere.

and then in a square...

They walked in a circle,

'FEE! FI! FO! FUM!'

A warty great ogre
who was wearing **bright shorts**
thrust a hairy great hand out—

And HELP they were caught!

Oh how they all trembled
as they hung in mid air
while the ogre stared hard
at the mouse, hare and bear!

'You think that I'll eat you
'cause I'm big and I'm strong,
but vegetarians believe
meat eating is wrong!'

PHEW!

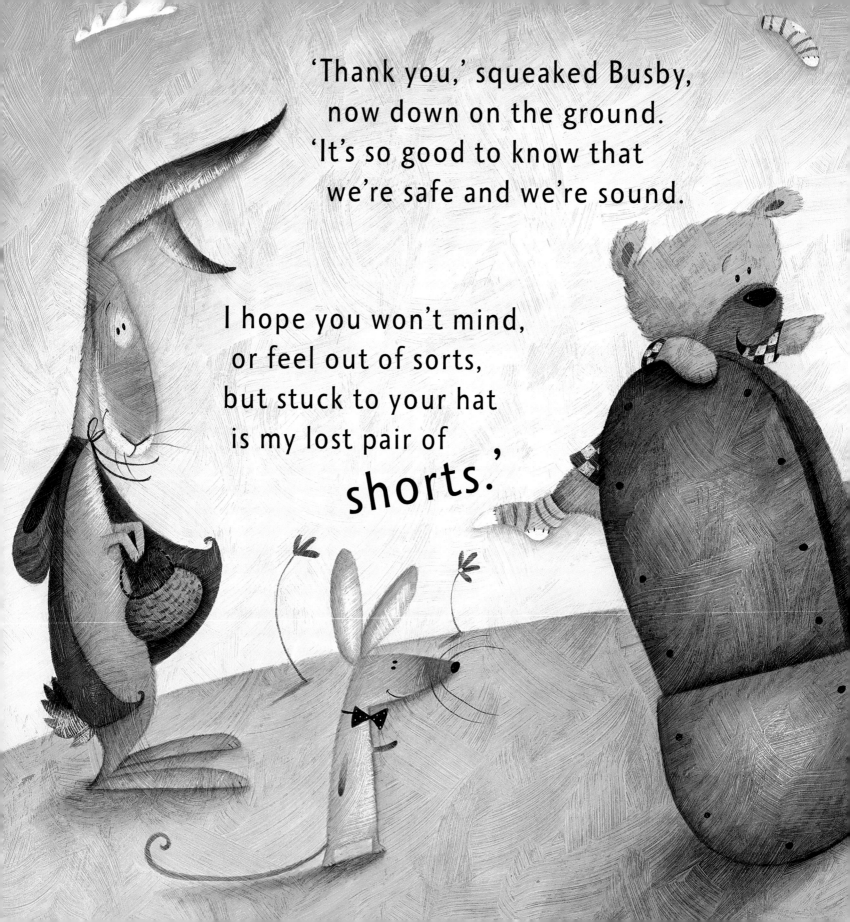

'Thank you,' squeaked Busby,
now down on the ground.
'It's so good to know that
we're safe and we're sound.

I hope you won't mind,
or feel out of sorts,
but stuck to your hat
is my lost pair of
shorts.'

'Ho! Ho! Ho!'

'You're joking!
You're kidding!
It's surely not so?'
And the ogre burst
out with a loud,

He pulled off the shorts,
'Yes, I see you're undressed!
You **are** short of clothes;
let me help find the rest.'

So the hare and the mouse
and the ogre with warts
walked hand in hand
with the bear wearing shorts.

They searched high and low. They looked everywhere. They walked in a circle...

...and
were
back
at bear's
lair!

Busby opened the door,
and was in for a shock,

because there by his shoes
lay one striped yellow sock!

Busby tied up his laces
and smoothed down his hair,
saying,

'Thank you my friends, now
I'm not a bare bear!'